Mystery at the museum.

The guide led the class to another dinosaur skeleton.

"This is the skeleton of the Coelophysis," the guide said. "Seel-o-fy-sis," she said again slowly.

Cam was busy studying the dinosaur's tail.

"Something is wrong," she whispered to Eric.

Cam closed her eyes and said, "Click." *She kept them closed for a while. Then she looked again at the dinosaur's tail.*

"I was right," Cam said to Eric. "Something is *wrong. Three of the dinosaur's bones are missing."*

THE CAM JANSEN ADVENTURE SERIES
David A. Adler/Susanna Natti

Cam Jansen and the Mystery of the Stolen Diamonds
Cam Jansen and the Mystery of the U.F.O.
Cam Jansen and the Mystery of the Dinosaur Bones
Cam Jansen and the Mystery of the Television Dog
Cam Jansen and the Mystery of the Gold Coins
Cam Jansen and the Mystery of the Babe Ruth Baseball
Cam Jansen and the Mystery of the Circus Clown
Cam Jansen and the Mystery of the Monster Movie
Cam Jansen and the Mystery of the Carnival Prize
Cam Jansen and the Mystery of the Monkey House
Cam Jansen and the Mystery of the Stolen Corn Popper
Cam Jansen and the Mystery of Flight 54
Cam Jansen and the Mystery at the Haunted House
Cam Jansen and the Chocolate Fudge Mystery
Cam Jansen and the Triceratops Pops Mystery
Cam Jansen and the Ghostly Mystery
Cam Jansen and the Scary Snake Mystery
Cam Jansen and the Catnapping Mystery
Cam Jansen and the Barking Treasure Mystery

CAM JANSEN
and the Mystery of the Dinosaur Bones

★★

DAVID A. ADLER
Illustrated by Susanna Natti

★★

PUFFIN BOOKS

To two wonderful people,
my parents

PUFFIN BOOKS
Published by the Penguin Group
Penguin Putnam Inc., 375 Hudson Street, New York, New York 10014, U.S.A.
Penguin Books Ltd, 27 Wrights Lane, London W8 5TZ, England
Penguin Books Australia Ltd, Ringwood, Victoria, Australia
Penguin Books Canada Ltd, 10 Alcorn Avenue, Toronto, Ontario, Canada M4V 3B2
Penguin Books (N.Z.) Ltd, 182-190 Wairau Road, Auckland 10, New Zealand

Penguin Books Ltd, Registered Offices: Harmondsworth, Middlesex, England

First published in the United States of America by The Viking Press, 1981
Published in Puffin Books, 1991
Reissued 1997

20 19 18 17 16 15

THE LIBRARY OF CONGRESS HAS CATALOGED THE PREVIOUS
PUFFIN EDITION UNDER CATALOG CARD NUMBER: 90-53367.
This edition ISBN 0-14-038715-3

Printed in the United States of America

RL: 2.4

Chapter One

"S*lurp.*"

Cam Jansen was drinking milk through a straw. She tilted the container to get the last few drops.

Cam was eating lunch in the cafeteria of the Kurt Daub Museum. She was there with her fifth-grade class. Her friend Eric Shelton was sitting next to her.

Cam pointed to the teacher. The teacher was standing on a chair with a finger over her mouth.

"Look," Cam said to Eric. "Ms. Benson is waiting for us to be quiet."

"Our tour will begin in twenty minutes," Ms. Benson said. "But first I must ask those of you who brought cameras along to keep your cameras in their cases. The

taking of photographs in the museum is not allowed."

Ms. Benson got down from the chair.

"See," Cam said to Eric, "I told you not to bring your camera. Last time I was here someone was told to leave the museum because he was taking pictures."

"Well," Eric said, "maybe I can't take pictures, but you can. Take a picture of me now with your mental camera."

Cam's mental camera is her memory. She can take one look at a page in a book, close her eyes, and remember every word on the page. "It's easy for me," Cam often explained. "I have a photograph of the page stored in my brain. When I want to remember what I saw, I just look at the photograph."

When people found out about Cam's amazing photographic memory, they stopped using her real name, Jennifer. They started calling her "The Camera."

Soon "The Camera" was shortened to "Cam."

Cam looked straight at Eric and said, "*Click.*" She always said, "*Click,*" when she wanted to remember something. Cam says that "*Click*" is the sound her mental camera makes when it takes a picture.

"Close your eyes," Eric said. "Now what do you remember?"

Cam thought for a moment. Then she said, "There's a drop of mustard on your collar. You should wipe it off!"

Eric looked down. There *was* a drop of mustard on his collar. He took a napkin and wiped it off.

"On the side of the milk container you just bought," Cam went on, "it says, 'Edna's. Our cows send you their love and their milk.'

"You're wearing a blue shirt. The top button of the shirt once came off and someone sewed it back on."

"You're right," Eric said. "But how did you know about the button?"

Cam opened her eyes. "It's the thread," she said. "I remembered that the top button was sewn on with white thread. The other buttons have light blue thread."

Ms. Benson was standing on a chair again. She said to the class, "Clean your tables and then get into a double line."

Cam and Eric quickly threw away the empty milk containers and the wrappings from their lunches. Then they got in line.

Ms. Benson led the class up the stairs to the museum lobby. They were met there by a young woman in a purple dress.

"I'm Janet Tyler," the woman in the purple dress said. "I will be your guide. Please stay together and follow me."

The guide led the class to the Air Travel room. She pointed out the models of the earliest flying machines. There was a full-size model of the 1903 Wright brothers' airplane.

Ms. Tyler took the class to a weather station room with a solar energy exhibit. Then she led the class into a large room with a very high ceiling.

AIR TRAVEL
LEONARDO DA VINCI

"This next exhibit is my favorite," the guide told the class.

"Mine, too," Cam whispered to Eric.

Chapter Two

The class followed the guide into the room. Glass cases filled with old tools, bones, rocks, and photographs lined the walls. On a platform, in the center of the room, was part of the skeleton of a very large dinosaur, the Brachiosaurus. Some of the bones from the skeleton were lying on the platform. The wires had come loose and the skeleton was being repaired.

"This is the skeleton of a Brachiosaurus. Brake-e-o-sawr-us," Janet Tyler said again slowly so everyone could hear how the word was pronounced. "The Brachiosaurus was the biggest dinosaur. It weighed over fifty tons. That's more, I'm sure, than all the children in your whole school weigh together."

Then the guide led the class to another dinosaur skeleton. It was much smaller than the Brachiosaurus. Its mouth was open and its hands were stretched out as if it were ready to grab something to eat.

"Look at those teeth," someone in the class said.

"And look at that tail. It's so long and pointy."

"This is the skeleton of a Coelophysis," the guide said. "Seel-o-fy-sis," she said again slowly. "Now you may know about some dinosaurs, but I'm sure no one knows anything about the Coelophysis."

"I do," Cam said.

Everyone turned to look at Cam. They were surprised that she knew about the

Coelophysis. Ms. Benson had never mentioned it when she taught the class about dinosaurs.

Cam had read about the Coelophysis. She wanted to remember exactly what the book said. She closed her eyes and said, "*Click.*"

When Cam said, "*Click,*" the guide started to laugh. She covered her mouth with her hand.

"The Coelophysis," Cam said with her eyes still closed, "was one of the first dinosaurs. It was about eight feet long, including its tail. It weighed no more than fifty pounds. It was a meat eater and . . ."

"Yes, thank you," the guide said before Cam had a chance to finish. "What you may not know is that these bones were discovered by Dr. Kurt Daub, the scientist who started this museum."

"Are people still finding dinosaur bones?" Eric asked.

"Yes," Ms. Tyler answered. "I'll be going on a dinosaur hunt in a few weeks, and I hope to find some myself."

Someone else asked, "Are all those bones real?"

"No. Dr. Daub didn't find a complete skeleton. Some of these bones were made from plaster of Paris."

There were many other questions, but Cam stopped listening. She was busy studying the dinosaur's tail.

"Something is wrong," she whispered to Eric.

Cam closed her eyes and said, "*Click.*" She kept them closed for a while. Then she

looked again at the dinosaur's tail.

"I was right," Cam said to Eric. "Something *is* wrong. Three of the dinosaur's bones are missing."

Chapter Three

Cam raised her hand and tried to get the museum guide's attention. But Ms. Tyler looked past her.

The guide pointed to a boy wearing a suit and a bow tie. "You have a question."

"I want to know why they are called dinosaurs."

Ms. Tyler smiled. "The name 'dinosaur' comes from two words, 'dino' which means 'terrible,' and 'saur' which means 'lizard.' So when we call them dinosaurs, we are really calling them terrible lizards."

"What did dinosaurs eat?" another boy asked.

"Some ate meat. Some ate plants, and some ate the eggs of other dinosaurs."

Then the guide looked at Cam. She smiled. "It seems that the red-haired girl, the one who says, '*Click,*' has a question."

"What happened to the tail?" Cam asked. "The last time I was here, it had three more bones. They were right here."

Cam pointed to the part of the tail near the hip. Farther down, there were bones that hung down from the tail like ribs. Where Cam pointed there weren't any bones.

"There's nothing missing on this dinosaur," the guide said quickly. "Now, are there any other questions?"

"But there *are* some bones missing. I've been here before and—"

"I'm here every day, and this skeleton

looks the same as it always does."

The guide answered a few other questions. Then she told Ms. Benson that the tour was finished, and she walked away.

Ms. Benson was a short woman. She stood on her toes so the whole class could see her.

"It's still early," Ms. Benson said. "You

have an hour to go through the museum by yourselves. At two-thirty all of you must be in the front lobby. If you don't have a watch, please stay near someone who does."

"Let's go to the gift shop," Eric said to Cam. "I want to buy presents for my twin sisters and my brother, Howie."

In the gift shop there were shelves of books and racks of postcards. Kits to make airplane models and models of dinosaurs were piled on a table with toys and games.

"All I have is a dollar," Eric said. "I hope I can find something."

While Eric looked around, Cam opened a big book called *Dinosaurs.* There was a whole page on the Coelophysis, but there was no illustration of its skeleton. The book told about how the Coelophysis hunted for food and how it might have looked, but it did not say how many bones the Coelophysis had in its tail.

"Look what I bought for the twins," Eric said a few minutes later. He reached into a bag and took out two small whistles, each in the shape of a Brachiosaurus. Cam took one of the whistles and blew into it. It was a dog whistle. It made a sound dogs could hear clearly, but Cam and Eric could hardly hear it.

"These whistles are for calling dogs," Cam said. "Why did you buy them? Your family doesn't have a dog."

"I know, but these whistles are also toy dinosaurs, and they're just twenty-nine cents each. Everything else costs too much."

Eric reached into the bag again and took out two postcards. "Look at these," he said. "This one is for Howie." It was a picture of a hot-air balloon. "And this one is for me." The second postcard had a picture of the Coelophysis skeleton.

"Let me see that," Cam said.

Cam looked at the postcard carefully. Then she closed her eyes and said, "*Click.*"

"This is it!" she said, waving the postcard. "This is the way the skeleton looked when I saw it the last time I was here. Let's go to the dinosaur room. You'll see. Some bones are missing."

Cam and Eric quickly walked through the museum.

"All right," Cam said when they stood in front of the Coelophysis skeleton. "You count the bones hanging from the tail of the skeleton. I'll count the ones on the postcard."

Cam counted the bones on the postcard a few times. Then she said, "I counted thirty-four on the tail. How many did you count?"

"Thirty-one."

Chapter Four

Cam looked at her watch. It was two-thirty.

"Come on, Eric," she said. "It's time to go."

Eric put the postcards and whistles in his pocket, and they went to meet the class in the lobby. Ms. Benson asked the class to line up. Then she led them to the school bus.

On the bus Cam and Eric talked about the missing dinosaur bones.

"Why would anyone want them?" Eric asked.

"And how could anyone steal the bones?" Cam added. "The skeleton is wired together. In the time it would take to unhook a bone, I'm sure someone would walk by and see what they were doing."

The bus stopped in the school parking lot. Ms. Benson stood up.

"It's after three o'clock," she said. "So you may all go home."

It was a warm spring day. Cam and Eric had ridden their bicycles to school that morning. They went to the rack behind the school to get their bicycles.

As Cam unlocked her bicycle, she said, "The bones can't be taken when the museum is open. There are too many people around then, and too many guards. It must be done after the museum closes. Let's go back there. Maybe we can find out what's going on."

"But the museum closes early today," Eric said. "We won't have any time to look around."

Cam put rubber bands over the cuffs of her pants to keep them from getting caught in the bicycle as she rode.

"All we have to look for is a place to hide," Cam said. "We don't have to be home until six today. We can stay in the dinosaur room after the museum closes and watch to see what happens."

Cam was already on her bicycle. She started to ride away before Eric could tell her that he didn't want to hide in the museum.

Eric got on his bicycle. He pedaled hard, but he couldn't catch up with Cam. By the time he locked his bicycle in front of the museum, Cam was halfway up the steps. He caught up with her in the dinosaur room.

A bell sounded.

"The museum closes in five minutes," a guard called out.

"Let's leave now," Eric said, "or we'll be locked inside."

Cam crawled under a glass case filled with photographs. Eric followed her.

Cam whispered to Eric, "You can leave if you want to, but I'm staying."

The bell sounded again.

From their hiding place Cam and Eric could see only the bottoms of the other exhibit cases and the feet of the dinosaur skeletons. A few people walked past the glass case, but all Cam and Eric could see were their legs. Then it was quiet.

"We did it," Cam said.

It was quiet for a while. But soon Cam and Eric heard footsteps. A man was walking from one case to the next. He stopped at Cam and Eric's case. Then he bent down and looked straight at Cam and Eric.

Chapter Five

It was one of the museum guards.

"Come with me," he said.

The guard led them out of the dinosaur room, through the museum lobby, to the office of the museum director. The guard knocked on the door and walked in. Cam and Eric followed him.

The walls of the office were covered with paintings of prehistoric animals. There were statues of famous scientists and large stuffed animals all over the room. Cam and

Eric couldn't find the director among all those paintings and statues.

"Didn't you hear the bell?" the director asked.

Then Cam and Eric saw him. He was sitting between a statue of a woman scientist and two stuffed owls.

"Yes, we heard the bell," Cam said. "But three dinosaur bones are missing. Someone is stealing bones from the tail of the Coelophysis skeleton, and we want to see who it is."

"That's impossible," the director said, stroking his beard. "Nothing is missing. But if you want to watch over the Coelophysis, you can come back tomorrow when the museum opens." Then he said to the guard, "Now please take these children to the door and make sure that this time they leave the museum."

Cam and Eric followed the guard to the front entrance. The guard opened the door with a key and let them out.

"Now what?" Eric asked.

"There's nothing we can do," Cam said. "We can't get back inside, so let's go home."

While Cam and Eric started to unlock their bicycles, a truck rode past them. It backed into the museum driveway. A sign painted on the side of the truck said, "Beth's Milk Tastes Best."

"That's strange," Cam said. "Milk is usually delivered early in the morning, not late in the afternoon."

A man in a white uniform got out of the truck. He was carrying an empty milk box.

"Maybe some of the milk went bad," Eric said, "and he's picking it up."

The milkman knocked on the garage door. The door opened and he went inside. He came out a few minutes later, carrying a large brown bag in the box. He put it in the truck.

"There's probably a whole bunch of containers of sour milk in that bag," Eric said.

Cam and Eric heard the door on the other side of the truck open and someone get inside, but they couldn't see who it was. Then the truck backed up. As the truck passed them, Cam read the sign again.

"There's something else that's strange about that truck," Cam said. She closed her eyes and said, *"Click."*

"The museum doesn't use Beth's milk. It uses Edna's. That's what it said on the milk container you bought in the cafeteria."

Cam got on her bicycle. She turned to Eric and said, “That man wasn’t picking up sour milk. He was picking up something else. Come on, let’s follow the truck.”

Chapter Six

The streets were crowded with cars. It was after four o'clock, and many people were driving home from work. Cam stayed on the right-hand side of the street. Eric rode behind her. The milk truck was already a block ahead. Cam and Eric pedaled hard to catch up.

As Cam pedaled, her bicycle made a loud "clicking" sound. The kickstand was loose, and one of the pedals hit it as it went around.

The milk truck made a right turn onto a

side street, but before Cam and Eric could reach the corner, Cam had to stop. The loose kickstand was in the way. It was impossible for Cam to pedal.

Eric got off his bicycle, too. He pushed the kickstand on Cam's bicycle back into place.

Cam said, "Thank you."

"You really need a new one," Eric told her.

Cam and Eric got on their bicycles again. When they reached the corner, they signaled and turned.

Cam looked ahead. A big brown dog was running along the sidewalk. A few cars were parked along the side of the street. But Cam couldn't see the milk truck. She stopped and waited for Eric.

"We've lost it," Cam said.

"Maybe not. I think I see a truck parked in the driveway of one of the houses on the next block. Maybe it's the milk truck."

Eric led Cam to a small brick house with a white wooden fence around it. The milk truck was parked in the driveway. No one was sitting inside the truck.

"They must have gone into the house," Cam said. She leaned her bicycle against the fence. "You stay here and watch for them," she told Eric. "I'll look around in the back."

There was a high window on the side of the garage. As Cam walked past the window, she heard voices. She looked for something to stand on so she could see inside.

Someone tapped her on the back. It was Eric.

"I locked the bicycles to the fence," he said. "I didn't want to wait out there alone."

Cam found an empty wooden milk box behind the house. She put the box right under the window, climbed up, and looked through.

There was a large table inside the garage. A few small bones and some larger ones were on the table. The milk box with the brown bag that they had seen the man put in the truck was there, too. A bag of plaster of Paris was on the floor near some boxes, and metal tubs and a wheelbarrow with a pickax and shovel in it.

"Get down," Eric whispered. "Someone will see you."

"There's no one there," Cam said. "But there is an open door. Maybe it leads into the house. I'll bet that's where they went."

Eric climbed up on the box.

"Look!" Eric said. "The three missing bones are on that table!"

Eric got off the box. He pulled on Cam's sleeve. "Get down," he said. "Let's go back now."

Cam didn't move. She kept looking through the window.

"We can call the museum," Eric said. "We can tell them we found their missing dinosaur bones."

"Someone is coming through the door," Cam said. "It's the Milkman."

Eric quickly climbed onto the box. Cam

and Eric watched the Milkman take the brown bag out of the box. The bag was tied with string. The Milkman tried to untie the knot. He couldn't.

"Why did you tie it so tight?" he called into the house.

"Use the scissors," a woman's voice answered.

The Milkman reached into one of the boxes. He took out a pair of scissors and cut the string.

"I wonder what could be in there," Eric whispered.

"It can't be a bone from the Coelophysis," Cam said quietly. "It's too big."

The Milkman tore open the side of the bag. There was something large and white inside. He took it out and carefully placed it on the table.

"Wow!" Eric said. "Look at the size of that bone."

"It must be from the Brachiosaurus,"

Cam said, "the one they were fixing in the museum."

The Milkman took out a ruler and measured the bone. He took a pad and pencil from his pocket and wrote on the pad. Then he looked at the bag of plaster of Paris.

"We need more plaster," he called into the house.

"Then let's go get it," the woman said.

The Milkman walked through the open door and into the house.

"They'll probably use the plaster of Paris to make a copy of the bone," Cam said. "They'll take the copy to the museum tomorrow and leave it there in place of the real one."

"But how do they get in and out of the museum?" Eric asked.

"And why do they want the bones?" Cam added.

Cam and Eric stopped talking. They heard the front door of the house open and then slam shut.

After a few minutes Cam whispered, "I didn't hear the truck drive away, but they should be gone by now. Let's take a look."

Cam walked quietly. Eric followed her. Cam peeked out past the edge of the garage wall. She saw that the truck was still in the driveway. And she saw something else.

"Our bicycles," Cam said. "What if *they* see them!"

Chapter Seven

"We sure did see your bicycles," a man said.

Cam turned. It was the Milkman. He was standing behind Eric.

"Janet!" the Milkman called.

A woman came out. She was wearing a purple dress. It was Janet Tyler, the museum guide.

"Well, well," she said. "Look who we have here. It's the Click, Click Girl and her friend."

The Milkman put a key into a lock at the side of the garage door. The lock was electric. He turned the key and the door opened.

The Milkman led Cam and Eric into the garage. He pressed a button on the wall. The garage door closed.

Janet Tyler and the Milkman started to argue. She pointed to the dinosaur bones on the table.

"It's all over. We'll have to give these back. And it's your fault. You should have made copies of the three small bones last night. Then these kids wouldn't have followed us."

"I'm not giving anything back. Not yet," the Milkman said. "We'll do just as we planned. We'll take the bones along on our dinosaur hunt. We'll bury them and then dig them up. *Then* we'll give the bones back to the museum."

Janet closed her eyes and said, "I can just see the newspaper headline: 'Janet Tyler discovers buried dinosaur bones and gives them to the museum.' I'll be famous. I'll speak to science groups all over the country. I'll make a fortune."

Cam pulled on Eric's sleeve and whispered, "This is our chance. Janet's eyes are closed. Take out the whistles you bought."

Eric reached into his pocket. He took out the two dog whistles shaped like dinosaurs. Cam took one of them.

"When I tell you to, blow the whistle," Cam whispered. "Blow it as hard as you can."

"Stop whispering," the Milkman said.

Janet opened her eyes. She seemed surprised to be in the garage with Cam, Eric, and the Milkman.

Then the Milkman told Cam and Eric, "Either you agree not to tell anyone about our plan, or we'll call the museum director. We'll put the bones in your bicycle baskets and tell the director you took them and we caught you."

Cam turned to whisper to Eric.

Janet Tyler smiled. "That's right," she said. "You talk it over with your friend."

"Quietly count to three," Cam whispered. "Then blow the whistle."

"One. . ."

Cam quickly turned around. She pressed the garage door button.

"Two. . ."

The garage door opened.

"Three."

Cam and Eric blew the whistles hard.

Janet could hardly hear the sounds the whistles made. But she knew what kind of whistles they were.

"Get the bones!" Janet yelled. "Get the bones before some dog comes and runs off with them."

She opened the door to the house. The Milkman picked up as many of the bones as he could carry.

"Quick, Eric!" Cam said. "Crawl under the table."

Chapter Eight

Cam and Eric crawled under the table and ran out of the garage. A big brown dog and two smaller dogs ran past them toward the garage.

Cam and Eric ran around the milk truck to the bicycles. Eric tried to open the lock. He turned the dial a few times.

"Hurry!" Cam said.

"I can't remember the combination."

Cam closed her eyes. She said, *"Click."* Then she thought for a moment.

Inside the house there was a noise. Someone was coming out.

"It's four, eighteen, thirty-six," Cam said.

Eric turned the knob. The lock opened. Cam and Eric got on their bicycles just as the Milkman ran out of the house.

"Stop!" he yelled.

"Let's go!" Cam said to Eric.

Cam looked both ways. No cars were coming. She quickly rode across the street. Eric followed her.

Just as they got across the street, they heard the door of the milk truck open and shut. The engine started.

Cam pedaled hard. As she pedaled, her bicycle made a loud clicking sound. She tried to keep pedaling, but she couldn't. The kickstand was in the way.

Cam got off her bicycle. Eric stopped, too. He came over to help.

"Hurry. The truck's coming," Cam said.

Eric pushed the kickstand back into place. They both got back on their bicycles.

Cam started pedaling again. The bicycle made a clicking sound, but not as loud as before.

Cam turned quickly and looked behind

her. Eric was pedaling hard. And the milk truck was right behind Eric.

Cam pedaled as hard as she could. The clicking sound became louder again, but Cam kept pedaling. She signaled and turned the corner. Eric followed her.

"Screech!"

"Honk! Honk!"

Cam stopped pedaling and turned to see what was happening. A car had turned the corner right in front of the milk truck. Both the driver of the car and the Milkman had slammed on their brakes.

"This is our chance," Cam told Eric.

Cam and Eric were riding on a busy street now. There were stores on both sides of the street.

Cam saw a narrow path on the side of a candy store. She rode down the path to the back of the store. Eric followed her.

"Good thinking," Eric said once they had stopped their bicycles. "When the Milkman turns the corner, he won't be able to find us."

Cam got off her bicycle. Then she told Eric, "You stay here and watch the bikes. I'm going inside to call the museum."

There was only one telephone in the store. A large man was using it. Cam opened the telephone book and looked for the museum's number.

"Do you have any shirts on sale?" the man was saying into the telephone. "Yes . . . Extra-large . . . I want a sky-blue shirt. But not a rainy day sky-blue. It should be a sunny day sky-blue."

Cam found the museum's number. She looked at it and said, "*Click.*" Then she took a coin from her pocket and waited to use the phone.

". . . and I need a green shirt," the man said into the telephone. "But not grass-green. It should be more like a traffic-light green . . ."

Eric came into the store. "I saw the milk truck. It rode right past me. The Milkman and Janet Tyler looked angry, but they didn't see me or the bicycles."

The man said, "Thank you very much." He hung up and left the booth.

Cam said, *"Click,"* to help her remember the museum's number. Then she dialed.

"Hello," Cam said into the telephone. "I'd like to speak to the director."

She waited.

"This is Jennifer Jansen," Cam said. "I'm the girl who was found hiding in the dinosaur room after the museum closed."

Cam told the director about the Milkman, Janet Tyler, and the dinosaur bones. She also told him the name and address of the candy store. "Yes, we'll wait here for you," Cam said, and then she hung up.

"The museum director is coming," Cam told Eric. "He said that after we left, he went to the dinosaur room. He looked at the skeletons and saw that some bones were missing. He said we should wait in front of the store with our bicycles. When he gets here, he'll follow us to the house."

Chapter Nine

Cam and Eric went behind the store to get their bicycles. Eric started turning the dial on the lock.

"Do you remember the combination?" Cam asked.

"Sure, I only forgot the last time because we were in such a hurry."

As Eric was turning the dial, Cam laughed and said, "You know, I don't think any dog would really be interested in those dinosaur bones. They're too old."

Cam and Eric walked their bicycles to the

front of the candy store. They waited for the museum director.

Soon a car drove up and stopped in front of the store. The car was just like the museum exhibits—very old. The director was at the wheel. He waved to Cam and Eric. They got on their bicycles. The director followed them in his car to the small brick house with the white wooden fence. The milk truck was in the driveway again.

"This is it," Cam told the director.

"You don't have to worry about the bones," the director said. "Since I know Janet stole them, she can't bury the bones and pretend to discover them. The bones are no good to her any more, so I'm sure she'll give them back without any trouble."

The museum director got out of his car. "Of course, she'll lose her job and I'll have to report her and her friend to the police. But they should have known that could happen when they took the bones."

The museum director shook hands with Cam and Eric. "I want to thank both of you for all your help," he said. "Before you go, you must tell me how you knew that some bones were missing. I pass those skeletons all the time, and I didn't notice anything."

Cam explained, "The last time I was at the museum, I took a picture of the dinosaur skeleton. When I looked at the picture, I knew some bones were missing."

"But our guards don't let anyone take photographs in the museum."

"Cam's camera is different," said Eric. "She doesn't need film or a flash. Cam's camera is her memory."

The director smiled. "Well, we certainly won't stop your memory from taking photographs." He buttoned his jacket, and then he asked, "Can you take one of me?"

Cam laughed. Then she looked straight at the museum director and said, *"Click."*

BETH'S

Who stole the Babe Ruth baseball?

When Cam got to the door she told the guard, "You have to stop him!"

"What are you talking about?"

"That boy in the green jacket. He was there when a valuable baseball was stolen. The baseball was in the exhibit, and I'm sure that boy took it. That's why he's in such a rush to get out of here."

"Just because he's leaving the hall doesn't mean he's a thief," the guard said.

The boy in the green jacket turned and saw Cam talking to the guard. He started to run. The boy ran around the corner of the building. He was out of sight.

"We'll never catch him now," Cam said.

THE CAM JANSEN ADVENTURE SERIES
DAVID A. ADLER/SUSANNA NATTI

Cam Jansen and the Mystery of the Stolen Diamonds
Cam Jansen and the Mystery of the U.F.O.
Cam Jansen and the Mystery of the Dinosaur Bones
Cam Jansen and the Mystery of the Television Dog
Cam Jansen and the Mystery of the Gold Coins
Cam Jansen and the Mystery of the Babe Ruth Baseball
Cam Jansen and the Mystery of the Circus Clown
Cam Jansen and the Mystery of the Monster Movie
Cam Jansen and the Mystery of the Carnival Prize
Cam Jansen and the Mystery of the Monkey House
Cam Jansen and the Mystery of the Stolen Corn Popper
Cam Jansen and the Mystery of Flight 54
Cam Jansen and the Mystery at the Haunted House
Cam Jansen and the Chocolate Fudge Mystery
Cam Jansen and the Triceratops Pops Mystery
Cam Jansen and the Ghostly Mystery
Cam Jansen and the Scary Snake Mystery

CAM JANSEN
and the Mystery of the Babe Ruth Baseball

★ ★

DAVID A. ADLER
Illustrated by Susanna Natti

★ ★

PUFFIN BOOKS

PUFFIN BOOKS
Published by the Penguin Group
Penguin Putnam Inc., 375 Hudson Street, New York, New York 10014, U.S.A.
Penguin Books Ltd, 27 Wrights Lane, London W8 5TZ, England
Penguin Books Australia Ltd, Ringwood, Victoria, Australia
Penguin Books Canada Ltd, 10 Alcorn Avenue, Toronto, Ontario, Canada M4V 3B2
Penguin Books (N.Z.) Ltd, 182-190 Wairau Road, Auckland 10, New Zealand

Penguin Books Ltd, Registered Offices: Harmondsworth, Middlesex, England

First published in the United States by The Viking Press, 1982
Published in Puffin Books, 1991
Reissued 1998

9 10

THE LIBRARY OF CONGRESS HAS CATALOGED THE PREVIOUS PUFFIN BOOKS
EDITION UNDER CATALOG CARD NUMBER: 91-53037
This edition ISBN 0-14-130090-6

Printed in the United States of America

RL: 2.7

To Bette and Simeon Guterman
with love

Chapter One

It was a Sunday afternoon at the end of May. Cam Jansen and her friend Eric Shelton were in the local community center. A hobby show was being held there, and Cam's parents had brought their collection of circus posters.

Cam's father fixed his bow tie. He looked at his watch and said, "It's almost time."

"You should go now, before you miss it," Cam's mother added.

Cam and Eric rushed to the clock corner, where there were more than twenty cuckoo

clocks hanging on the wall. It was almost four o'clock. Cam and Eric waited. Then the noise started. When the minute hand of each clock reached twelve, a tiny door opened and a small wooden bird popped out. "Cuckoo, cuckoo, cuckoo, cuckoo," it chirped.

All the birds seemed to be coming out of all the clocks at once. People in the large room turned to look at the clocks. Many of them looked at their watches to see if it really was four o'clock.

After the clock doors had closed, Cam and Eric looked at some of the other exhibits. They looked at needlepoint pillows, the Collins Coin Shop exhibit, a display of old toys, and at a large collection of baseball cards, yearbooks, and posters.

"Look here," Eric said. "There's a whole section about Babe Ruth."

There were a few Babe Ruth baseball cards, some photographs, a baseball the

Babe had autographed, and a large poster of Babe Ruth hitting a home run. The poster also listed his record as a player.

"Test my memory," Cam told Eric. "Ask me anything about Babe Ruth's playing record."

Cam looked carefully at all the numbers on the poster. Then she closed her eyes and said, *"Click."* Cam always says, *"Click,"* when she wants to remember something. When people ask her why, she points to her head and tells them, "This is a mental camera. Just like any camera, it goes '*click*' when it takes a picture."

"What was the Babe's real name?" Eric asked.

"George Herman Ruth," Cam said with her eyes still closed.

"How many games did he play in 1924?"

"One hundred and fifty-three."

Cam has what people call a photographic memory. Her mind takes a picture of whatever she sees. When she wants to remember something, even a detail such as how many games Babe Ruth played in any

one year, she just looks at the photograph stored in her brain.

Cam's real name is Jennifer Jansen. But when people found out about her amazing memory, they called her "The Camera." Soon "The Camera" was shortened to "Cam."

"When did Babe Ruth get the most hits?" Eric asked.

"In 1923. He had two hundred and five hits that year. And he hit the most home runs in 1927. That's when he hit sixty," Cam said, with her eyes still closed.

The owner of the collection was listening. He was an old man. He had a bushy white mustache, and he was wearing a baseball cap.

"You really know all about baseball," the old man said.

Cam opened her eyes and said, "No, I don't. I just remember everything on that poster."

P.T. BARA
The

Then Eric told him, "She has a mental camera. Why don't you test her?"

The old man picked up a box of baseball cards. "Take a card," he called to the people around the exhibit. "We'll see how good this girl's memory *really* is."

Two people reached into the box and took out a card. Cam looked at the people. Then she looked at the cards they were holding. She said, *"Click,"* and closed her eyes.

"What card am I holding?" a teenage boy wearing jeans and a bright green jacket asked.

"You're holding a Reggie Jackson card."

"That's right," the boy said. Then he looked at his card and asked, "How many doubles did he hit in 1977?"

"Thirty-nine."

A girl with long brown hair, holding a large gym bag, asked, "What card am I

holding? When was the player born and what's his middle name?"

"It's a Stan Musial card. He was born in 1920, on November twenty-first, and his full name is Stanley Frank Musial."

"Amazing!" the man said as Cam opened her eyes. He told her that his name was Henry Baker, and he asked Cam and Eric if they could come back later. He wanted his wife to meet Cam and test her memory.

"Sure, I can come back," Cam told him.

"Oh, good. Now let me show you my collection."

Mr. Baker showed Cam and Eric his favorite baseball cards. He showed them cards of Billy Martin, Fernando Valenzuela, Ron Guidry, and Satchel Paige. After that, he led Cam and Eric to the Babe Ruth corner.

He showed them his Babe Ruth cards. Then Mr. Baker said, "Wait till you see

this. I have a baseball that Babe Ruth signed for me almost fifty years ago."

Mr. Baker turned around. The wooden stand the baseball had rested on was there, but the baseball was gone.

Chapter Two

"Someone stole my baseball!" Mr. Baker cried out.

A woman nearby looked at him. She laughed and said, "Ask your mommy to get you another one."

"This wasn't just any baseball. Babe Ruth signed it. He gave it to me when I was a boy. It's very valuable."

Mr. Baker ran from one person to the next, asking, "Have you seen my baseball? Did you see it rolling on the floor? Did you see someone take it?"

Eric looked on the floor for the ball. Cam stood on a chair to watch what Mr. Baker was doing.

"He's so upset," Cam told Eric. "He's stopping everyone. Most of them think he's crazy."

While Cam stood on the chair, she looked across the exhibit hall. She saw her parents with a large circus poster hanging behind them. She saw the wall of cuckoo clocks. Then she saw someone leaving the exhibit hall. It was a teenage boy wearing a bright green jacket. Cam closed her eyes and said, *"Click."*

"Let's go!" Cam shouted to Eric when she opened her eyes. "Someone's leaving the hall, and he might have the baseball."

Cam ran between two women trading rare postage stamps. She crawled under a few tables and almost knocked over a small boy looking at some old toys.

Eric followed Cam. "I'm sorry. Excuse me," he said to the two women and the small boy as he hurried past.

When Cam got to the door she told the guard, "You have to stop him!"

"What are you talking about?"

"That boy in the green jacket. He was

there when a valuable baseball was stolen. The baseball was in the exhibit, and I'm sure that boy took it. That's why he's in such a rush to get out of here."

"Just because he's leaving the hall doesn't mean he's a thief," the guard said.

The boy in the green jacket turned and saw Cam talking to the guard. He started to run.

"Did you see that!" Eric said. "He saw us talking to you and he started to run."

The boy ran around the corner of the building. He was out of sight.

"We'll never catch him now," Cam said.

"Yes, we will," the guard said.

He ran after the boy. Cam and Eric followed him.

They ran to a crowded playground on the other side of the building. Two young children were playing catch with a baseball. Others were jumping rope or playing basketball. In one corner of the playground some parents were watching very young children playing in a large sandbox, on seesaws, or on swings.

The guard ran with Cam and Eric until they got to the other end of the playground.

"He's gone," Cam said. "I don't see him anywhere."

They looked down the street leading

from the playground. A few children were walking there. A man was pushing a baby carriage, and there were some people waiting at the bus stop. But no one was wearing a bright green jacket.

"There's another way out of the playground," the guard said. He turned and started to walk toward the other exit. Then he stopped.

"Is that him?" the guard asked, pointing to a boy sitting on one of the park benches.

Chapter Three

The boy sitting on the bench was wearing jeans and a bright green jacket. He was sitting behind the two children who were playing catch.

"Yes, that's him," Cam said.

Cam, Eric, and the guard ran to the bench. The boy looked up at them. He smiled and said, "Well, look who's here. It's the girl with the amazing memory and her quiet friend."

"A valuable baseball is missing from one

of the exhibits," the guard told the boy. "We're looking for it."

"I'm sorry, but I don't know where it is."

Cam looked at the boy. There was something in one of his jacket pockets. It was round and about the size of a baseball.

Cam closed her eyes and said, *"Click."* She looked at the picture in her mind of the boy when he was holding the Reggie Jackson baseball card.

Cam opened her eyes and said, "What's that in your pocket? It wasn't there before."

"Oh, this," the boy said, and reached into his pocket. "You just didn't notice it."

He took out a baseball and showed it to the guard.

"This can't be the missing baseball," the guard said. "It's not signed by Babe Ruth. It says 'Little League Slugger.' "

The guard turned to Cam and Eric and said, "I don't know why I listened to you. Maybe there never was any Babe Ruth baseball. Now I have to get back to the exhibit hall. But first I think you owe this boy an apology."

Cam and Eric told the boy that they were sorry. The guard walked back to the exhibit hall. Cam and Eric walked to a bench on the other side of the playground and sat down.

Cam and Eric lived next door to each

other. They were in the same fifth grade class, and they spent a lot of time together. Eric knew that Cam wouldn't give up the search for the missing baseball so quickly. She didn't.

"Where did he get that ball? He didn't have it when we saw him at Mr. Baker's exhibit."

"Maybe he found it," Eric said.

"Maybe."

Cam closed her eyes. She said, *"Click."* Then she added, "I'm trying to remember everything I saw at the exhibit."

While Cam's eyes were closed, Eric looked around the playground. He saw a side door to the exhibit hall open.

"Cam, look! Isn't that the girl we saw at Mr. Baker's exhibit?"

Cam opened her eyes. She looked at the girl leaving the exhibit hall. The girl had long brown hair and was carrying a gym bag.

"Yes. That's her. And there's enough room in that gym bag for twenty baseballs. I'll bet she left through the side door so no one would see her."

The girl walked past Cam and Eric, but she didn't notice them. She walked out of the playground. At the corner she crossed the street and walked toward the bus stop.

"Come on," Cam said. "Let's follow her."

Cam and Eric had to wait at the corner for the traffic light to turn green. As they waited, the girl got farther and farther ahead. When the light changed, Cam and Eric ran to get closer. The girl turned and saw them. She began running, too.

The girl held the gym bag with both hands as she ran. She ran past the bus stop. She turned and saw Cam and Eric behind her. She looked scared.

At the corner the girl quickly looked to see if any cars were coming. Then she ran across the street.

"Let's rest," Eric said to Cam when they reached the corner.

"No. We have to catch her. I'm sure she took the baseball. That's why she's running."

Cam and Eric crossed the street and chased the girl. She was halfway down the block when her gym bag dropped from her

hands. The girl tripped over the bag and fell.

Cam and Eric caught up with the girl. She was still lying on the sidewalk. The girl held her gym bag up and said, “Here, take what you want. Just don’t hurt me.”

Chapter Four

"We're not going to hurt you," Eric told the girl.

Cam took the bag from the girl's hands and said, "We're just going to take the Babe Ruth baseball you stole and give it back to Mr. Baker."

"I didn't steal any baseball."

"Then why were you running?"

"I was running because you were chasing me."

"We'll see," Cam said as she opened the bag.

"Wait," Eric said. "It's her bag. We can't look through it unless she says we can."

The girl sat up and said, "Look all you want. You'll see that I didn't steal anything."

Cam reached into the bag. She took out an old newspaper, a puzzle book about outer space, and a dried-up slice of cheese.

"You should really wrap cheese in plastic or foil," Eric told the girl.

Cam reached into the bag again and took out an apple, an empty soda can, and a roller skate. She felt along the bottom of the bag.

"There's no baseball in here, but there sure are a lot of papers."

"Maybe my book report is in there. I wrote it last week, but I can't remember where I put it."

Eric helped the girl up. Cam gave the gym bag back to her and said, "I'm sorry we chased you. And I'm sorry we thought you stole that baseball."

"That's all right," the girl said as she looked through the papers in her bag. "It will be worth it if I find that book report."

The girl took old comic books, crushed homework papers, and candy wrappers from the bag. Cam and Eric left her and started walking toward the exhibit hall. When they reached the corner, the girl

waved some papers at them and called out, "I found it! I found it!"

"I'm glad we helped find *something*," Cam said to Eric. "But I wish it had been the baseball."

When Cam and Eric reached the playground, they sat down on one of the benches. Eric watched the children playing basketball.

Cam closed her eyes and said, "*Click.*" She thought for a moment. She said, "*Click,*" a few more times. Then she opened her eyes.

"The baseball was there when we first came to the exhibit, but it was gone a few minutes later. So it must have been taken while we were there," Cam said. "I just wish I had a picture of who was standing in the Babe Ruth corner when the ball was taken."

Eric wasn't looking at Cam while she talked to him. He was looking across the playground.

"The one thing that I don't understand," Eric said, "is why that boy ran from the hall. He was in a real hurry then, but he didn't go anywhere. He's still sitting there on that bench."

Cam looked across the playground. Then she closed her eyes and said, "*Click.*"

Cam told Eric, "I'm looking at the picture

I have of him at the exhibit. He said he had a baseball in his pocket the whole time, but that's not true. He didn't have it in his pocket when we first saw him."

Cam opened her eyes and asked, "What is he doing over there?"

"It looks like he's watching those two children playing catch."

Cam looked across the playground at the boy in the green jacket. She thought for a minute. Then she clapped her hands together and said, "That's it! I think I know where the Babe Ruth baseball is."

"Where?"

Cam started to explain, but then she saw something that made her stop.

"Look at that," she said, and pointed across the playground. "Now I *know* where the baseball is."

Chapter Five

Cam was pointing to the two children playing catch. One of them had thrown the ball too far. The boy in the green jacket was picking it up.

"Did you see that?" Cam asked.

"See what?"

"He picked up their baseball. Now I bet he'll switch baseballs. He'll throw back the one he has in his pocket."

The boy in the green jacket turned around. As he turned, he took the baseball out of his pocket and threw it over his head

to the two children. Then he started to walk away.

"Come on, Eric. Let's follow him."

"Why? What's the difference if he did switch baseballs? Those children couldn't have the Babe Ruth ball. They were outside when it was stolen."

The boy in the green jacket walked quickly away from the playground. He didn't even look as he crossed the street.

Horns honked. Two cars stopped short to avoid hitting him. But the boy didn't even turn around.

Cam ran through the playground and out the exit. Eric followed her. They waited at the corner and then crossed the street when they were sure no cars were coming. The boy was almost a full block ahead of them.

"Let's be careful," Cam told Eric. "I don't want that boy to know we're following him."

Cam and Eric stayed about half a block behind the boy. They walked past a row of stores. At the corner the boy turned around. He looked straight at Cam and Eric.

"Quick!" Cam said. "Let's go into one of these stores."

It was Sunday. The only place open was a small food store. Cam opened the door, and Eric quickly followed her inside.

"Can I help you?" a man behind the counter asked.

"No. We don't need anything," Cam told him.

"Of course you do. Now try to remember what your mother sent you to get. Was it milk? We have regular milk, ninety-nine-

percent-fat-free milk, skim milk, and buttermilk."

"We don't need milk," Eric said.

"Maybe you came for bread or canned vegetables. We have peas, spinach, corn, carrots, and lima beans."

Cam opened the door and looked outside. Then she told Eric, "Let's go before we lose him."

"Maybe you need juice," the man called as Cam and Eric were leaving. "We have orange juice, apple juice, tomato juice, grapefruit juice, and lemon juice."

When Cam and Eric stepped outside the store, they looked for the boy. He was gone. They ran to the corner. They looked ahead and down both side streets.

"There he is," Eric said.

The boy was walking down one of the side streets. Cam and Eric were careful not to get too close. There were a few stores along the first half of the block. The rest of

the block was lined with apartment buildings. They saw the boy walk into one of the buildings.

Cam and Eric ran to the building. They peeked into the lobby. The boy was standing there waiting for the elevator. He got into the elevator, and the doors closed behind him.

Cam and Eric ran into the building. They watched the numbers over the elevator door light up. Number five stayed lit for a long time.

"He got off on the fifth floor," Cam told Eric. "Now we know where he lives. I'll stay here and watch to make sure he doesn't leave. You go get the police."

"No!"

"No?"

"You still haven't told me why we followed him. What will I tell the police?"

Cam sat on one of the chairs in the lobby. Eric sat next to her.

"While we were sitting in the playground, I looked at the pictures I have stored in my head. That boy didn't have a ball in his pocket when we first saw him at the exhibit. But he did have one when we saw him later."

"But it wasn't the Babe Ruth baseball."

"I know it wasn't. At first that confused me. Then I saw a ball get away from those two children playing catch. When the boy picked it up, I knew what had happened."

"What?"

"That boy took the Babe Ruth ball from the exhibit. He saw us speaking to the guard so he ran. But then he had a better idea. The ball the two children were playing with must have landed near him. That was the first time he switched the baseballs. The two children didn't know it, but they were playing catch with a very valuable baseball."

Eric stood up and said, "Then, while we were watching, he switched the baseballs again. Now he has the Babe Ruth ball."

Eric walked toward the door. As he was leaving the building, he said to Cam, "You wait right here. I'll go and get the police."

"And tell my parents where I am," Cam said.

Cam waited until she was sure that Eric was gone. Then she walked over and pushed the button for the elevator. When it came, she got on and pressed the button for the fifth floor.

Chapter Six

The elevator stopped on the third floor. A woman was standing there reading a flier about the items on sale at the local supermarket. She got into the elevator and asked, "Are you going down?"

"No. I'm going up," Cam answered.

The woman smiled and said, "That's all right. I'll come along for the ride."

The doors closed and the elevator started to move.

The elevator stopped on the fifth floor and Cam got off. The hall was lined with

doors. *What will I tell the police?* Cam wondered. *How will they know which is the boy's apartment?*

Cam looked at the names on each of the doors: Benson, Jackson, Goldwin, Cruz, Washington, Hamada, Grant, and Keller.

Maybe his name is Benson, Cam thought. *He looked like a Benson. Or maybe he's a Keller.*

A door opened. It was the door to the Goldwin apartment. As the door opened, a

paper fell to the floor. It was a flier just like the one the woman in the elevator had had. Cam looked at a few of the other apartment doors. Each one had a folded flier pressed into the frame of the door.

A tall woman with red hair just like Cam's came out of the Goldwin apartment. Two children were with her. One of the children, a small boy with curly blond hair, picked up the flier. As they walked to the elevator, the woman smiled at Cam.

Cam waited until they were in the elevator. Then she walked from one apartment door to the next. Two of them, the Goldwins' and the Grants', did not have fliers.

His name is Grant, Cam said to herself. *He must have taken the flier when he went inside.*

Cam was just about to knock on the door when she heard some people get off the elevator. It was Cam's parents and Eric, with a policeman and a policewoman.

"Why didn't you wait for us downstairs?" Eric asked.

"His name is Grant," Cam told them. "This is his apartment."

"What were you about to do?" Cam's father asked.

"I hope you weren't going to knock on the door," Cam's mother said. "Chasing and catching a thief isn't something children should do. It's a job for the police."

The policeman knocked on the door.

"Who is it?" a voice called from inside the apartment.

"It's the police. We'd like to ask a few questions."

The door was opened by a boy wearing jeans.

"Is this the boy you think took the baseball?" the policeman asked.

"Yes," Cam told him.

"No!" the boy shouted. "You're wasting your time. This is the second time these

two kids have said I stole that baseball. I had one with me when I left the exhibit, but it wasn't the Babe Ruth ball. I showed it to them the last time."

"Would you please show it to us?" the policewoman asked.

"Just a minute."

The boy opened a closet near the front door of the apartment. Then he held out a baseball.

Cam looked at the ball. She closed her eyes and said, *"Click."*

"This isn't the same one you showed us in the park," Cam said when she opened her eyes.

"Is this the Babe Ruth baseball?" the policewoman asked.

"No."

"Then let's go."

The boy was just closing the apartment door when something green caught Cam's eye. The boy's jacket was hanging over the back of a kitchen chair. And there was something on the kitchen table.

"Wait," Cam said. "Don't close the door."

Chapter Seven

Cam's father held the door open.

"What is it now?" the policewoman asked Cam.

"I saw the baseball. It's on the kitchen table."

"Are you sure?"

"I think I'm sure."

The policewoman looked inside the apartment. "Oh, there *is* a baseball on the table," she said. "Bring it here," she told the boy.

The boy walked slowly to the kitchen. He

took the baseball off the table and brought it to the policewoman.

"It sure is old," the policewoman said as she looked at the ball. "And it says here 'To Henry Baker, from The Babe.' "

"Maybe it's mine," the boy said.

"Is it?" the policewoman asked.

"Well, no," the boy said softly. "I took it from the old man. I'm sorry."

"You'll have to come to the police station with us. We'll call your parents," the policewoman said as she led the boy to the elevator.

"But first we'll stop at the exhibit," the policeman said. "We'll return the baseball to Mr. Baker."

They all squeezed into the police car. The boy just stared quietly out of the car window. But the police officers and Cam's parents weren't quiet at all. They talked all during the ride to the exhibit hall.

"I'm too young to remember the great

Babe Ruth," the policewoman said. "But my father told me lots of stories about him.

"His favorite story was about the time Babe Ruth hit a home run in the 1932 World Series. The score was tied. There were two strikes. The Babe pointed to the centerfield fence. Then . . ." She paused.

"And then what happened?" asked Cam's mother.

"That's where he hit the very next pitch, right over the centerfield fence."

"And on the *next* pitch," the policeman said, "Lou Gehrig hit a home run."

"He was a pretty good ballplayer, too," Cam's father said.

When they reached the exhibit hall, Cam, her parents, Eric, and the policewoman went inside. Cam held the baseball with both hands.

Mr. Baker was sitting in the Babe Ruth corner of the exhibit. His head was down.

Eric tapped him on the shoulder. Then Cam gave him the baseball.

"You found it! You found it!" Mr. Baker yelled. He hugged Cam, Cam's father, Eric, the policewoman, and a man who just happened to be walking past.

"Look, they found my baseball!" Mr.

Baker told his wife when she came from the other side of the exhibit.

"I'm not putting this back on display," Mr. Baker said as he put the baseball in his pocket. "Someone else might take it."

"I want you to come to the station house and sign a complaint against the boy who took it," the policewoman said. "Come as soon as the exhibit closes."

The policewoman started to leave.

"Wait," Mr. Baker said. He took a handful of baseball cards from the box. "Take this," he said as he handed the policewoman a card. "It's Hank Aaron. He's the greatest home run hitter of all time. And here's George Brett and Yogi Berra and Willie Mays and Pete Rose."

The policewoman held up her hands and said, "Oh, thank you, but don't give them to me. Give them to these two children. They're the ones who found your baseball."

Mr. Baker gave the cards to Cam and Eric.

"Can you stay a little longer?" he asked Cam. "My wife would like to see you and your amazing mental camera at work."

"Sure."

"Good. Wait right here. I want everyone to see what a great memory you have."

Chapter Eight

"May I have your attention, please," a woman's voice called out over the loudspeaker. "First, I want to thank you for coming to our hobby show. And I want to invite all of you to go to Henry Baker's baseball exhibit. An amazing memory show will be given there in just a few minutes."

A small crowd gathered around Mr. Baker's exhibit. Cam's parents stood right near the front. Both of them were tall and thin. Cam's father had red hair just like

Cam. Cam's mother's hair was brown and curly.

Mr. Baker and Cam were standing on chairs. Mr. Baker quietly asked Cam a few questions. Then he announced, "The girl standing next to me is Jennifer Jansen. She is in the fifth grade, and she has a remarkable memory."

Mr. Baker picked up a box and said, "I'm going to pick a few cards from this box. Jennifer will take a quick look at the cards. Then I'll let you test her memory."

Mr. Baker picked out some cards and handed them to Cam. Cam said, "*Click,*" as she looked at each card. Then she gave the cards to Eric and closed her eyes.

Eric gave the cards to people in the crowd. "Ask her anything you want," Eric told them.

"I'm holding a Dave Winfield card," someone called out. "What's his middle name?"

The BABE

"Mark."

"What's Eddie Murray's hobby?"

"Basketball."

A woman standing next to Cam's parents said, "She sure has an amazing memory."

Cam's mother told the woman, "She's our daughter. We're very proud of her."

"And not just because of her memory," Cam's father said. "We were proud of her even before she said her first *'Click.'* "